# Starring Me!

Cathy Miyata

Illustrations by
Susan Gardos

Scholastic Canada Ltd.

*Thank you to Sylvia McNicoll and Lynda Simmons*
*for their enormous generosity,*
*and Ashley Taylor for her technical advice on*
*professional children's theatre.*

**Canadian Cataloguing in Publication Data**

Miyata, Cathy, 1956–
　　Starring me!

ISBN 0-590-51532-2

I. Title.

PS8576.I92S72 1999　　　　jC813'.54　　　　C99-930532-8
PZ7.M699576St 1999

7 6 5 4 3　　　　　　　Printed in Canada　　　　　　　2 3/0

# Starring Me!

## Cathy Miyata

SHOOTING STAR

SCHOLASTIC

# Starring Me!

**Have you read these Shooting Star books?**

- ❏ *Aliens in the Basement* • Suzan Reid

- ❏ *The Big Race!* • Sylvia McNicoll

- ❏ *A Ghost in the Attic* • Suzan Reid

- ❏ *Howard's House is Haunted* • Maureen Bayless

- ❏ *Liar, Liar, Pants on Fire* • Gordon Korman

- ❏ *The Lost Locket* • Carol Matas

- ❏ *Monsters in the School* • Martyn Godfrey

- ❏ *Princesses Don't Wear Jeans* • Brenda Bellingham

- ❏ *Project Disaster* • Sylvia McNicoll

- ❏ *School Campout* • Becky Citra

- ❏ *Sleepover Zoo* • Brenda Kearns

- ❏ *Worm Pie* • Beverly Scudamore

# Contents

*For my mother, Reverend Elizabeth Aitken,*
*the most inspirational person I know.*

# Chapter 1

# Everyone's Looking at Me!

Mr. Cowles whacked his pencil on the edge of my desk. *Tap. Tap. Tap.*

The whispers around the room faded away until it was prickly quiet. I swallowed hard. The last time Mr. Cowles tapped his pencil he made Clayton Pratt apologize to the whole class. Clayton had said dirty words outside at recess.

Uh oh. Did someone tell Mr. Cowles that I called Clayton a dweeb this morning? Was that a bad word?

I glanced over at Clayton. His yellow hair hid his eyes, but I could see his teeth. He was grinning like a cartoon bear. He was happy that Mr. Cowles was tapping on my desk. I clamped my teeth together tight.

"Stand up, Ashley," Mr. Cowles prompted. We always have to stand in Mr. Cowles' class.

I looked up at Mr. Cowles.

"Don't you have something to tell the class?" he asked me quietly.

I pushed myself up from my chair. My knees felt spongy. I looked over at my best pal Krystal. Her face was so red it made her black braids look blue. Her cheeks were bulging like she had stuffed her mouth with ping-pong balls. She was holding her breath. She always held her breath when she was nervous and right now I could tell she was nervous for me. But her ping-pong cheeks made me not quite so scared.

"Ashley?"

I looked back up at Mr. Cowles. I opened my mouth but nothing came out.

Mr. Cowles pushed his big glasses down to the end of his nose. One of his eyes closed and quickly opened again.

Had Mr. Cowles just winked at me?

"No need to be shy, Ashley. I'm sure everyone wants to know." He lowered his voice. "Your mother phoned the school this morning, and the principal just told me your news."

"Oh, *that!*" I exploded. I straightened up and lifted my head. Everyone was staring at me. A little tingle ran up my spine. It was like someone had swallowed a mouthful of air from the freezer and sent it whooshing down my back.

I looked around. Clayton Pratt was quiet. Waiting. Everyone was waiting. The tingly feeling snuck down my arms. My fingers felt like fizzy-pop candies.

Hey, this was neat. I had everyone's attention without even saying a word!

"I . . . got a part in *Joseph* . . . the musical . . . you know . . . *Joseph and the Amazing Technicolor Dreamcoat*, in the city. Starring Brandon Colt."

"You?" Clayton blurted. "And Brandon Colt?"

I smiled and nodded.

"Wow!" Julia breathed.

"Will you actually meet him?"

"Can we come?"

"When do you start?"

"Do you get paid?"

"Will you be on television?"

"Are you a star?"

"One question at a time!" Mr. Cowles interrupted.

Hands shot up all over the room.

"You answer them, Ashley, it's your show."

Answer questions? It wasn't even Sharing Time.

I looked over at Krystal. She was smiling as bright as a star. But she wasn't a star. She was just happy for me.

Krystal had wanted to try out for *Joseph* too, but her mom said no. Krystal's dad moved away a few months ago and her mom started working all day. Now Krystal has to help look after her little brother and sister after school. Too bad. She would have gotten a part for sure, because she sings alone sometimes for her church choir and she sounds really good. We could have been standing up in front of the class together.

I gave Krystal a thumbs-up, then looked around at all of the other faces. Their eyes were big, their mouths open. The tingly feeling grew until it crept over my hair and all the way down to my toes.

I moved away from my desk and pointed at Sabrina first. Everyone liked Sabrina. She had cool Doc Martens shoes. She wore a jean jacket with shiny jewels on the collar, that really belonged to her older sister. And now she was asking me questions.

I pushed back my hair and smiled my best smile. I imagined my short brown hair

shining. I could see my teeth sparkling like I was in a bright light on a big stage. The star.

# Chapter 2

# Putting On a Real Play

When I finally sat down, everyone clapped. Clapped! And I hadn't even done anything yet. My cheeks were sore from smiling so much, but I didn't care.

"This is the perfect time for my announcement," said Mr. Cowles. We all sat very still, listening. "We are going to put on a play in our class and everyone gets to be in it."

Some of the kids groaned, but most of the

girls squealed and waved their arms like the teenagers on MusicTV.

"Can it be *Joseph*?" called out Sabrina.

"No," said Mr. Cowles.

"Aww!" everyone whined.

"And please remember to raise your hand."

Sabrina pouted. I just smiled some more. They wanted to be in my play.

"We will present *The Wizard of Oz*," Mr. Cowles announced proudly.

"Ohh," everyone moaned.

Everyone except Krystal. I looked at her as soon as Mr. Cowles said it. She clasped her hands together and beamed. *The Wizard of Oz* is Krystal's favourite movie. She knows every song by heart. She's always singing "Somewhere Over the Rainbow." I think it's a dumb show, but Krystal has loved it since she was little.

Sabrina put her hand up. Mr. Cowles nodded at her.

"Mr. Cowles, that's a movie. Maybe we should make a movie, too."

"Yes, Sabrina, it is. But we are not making a movie. We are putting on a play. And our play will be different from the movie, you'll see."

The class was quiet. I could tell they were not happy. They did not want to put on Krystal's favourite show. Krystal's hands dropped into her lap and her smile faded. I had to do something quick, before Mr. Cowles changed his mind. I shot up my hand.

Mr. Cowles smiled at me and nodded. He definitely liked me more now that I was a star.

"Mr. Nielson — he's my director — last night he told everyone in our cast that *live* theatre is better than movies. He said it takes *real* talent to be in a play. And *The Wizard of Oz* is a famous pla — he told us he even directed it once." I crossed my arms and nodded so hard my hair bounced and everyone nodded too.

Julia put up her hand now.

"Yes, Julia?" said Mr. Cowles.

"Is it dangerous to be in a play?" Her voice was soft.

"Well, no. Why do you ask?" Mr. Cowles'

eyebrows squeezed together and so did mine.

"Ashley said everyone in her play is wearing a cast. Will I break something too?"

"Ohhhh, Julia!" most of the kids moaned.

Mr. Cowles looked over at me. He had a big grin on his face. "Go ahead Ashley, you explain," he said.

"A *cast* is what you call everyone *in* the play," I said slowly and loudly. I looked around at all the kids. Some nodded. Some still looked confused, including Krystal.

I sighed. "It's all right, Mr. Cowles, I'll explain it some more at recess." Mr. Cowles and I had a lot of work to do, that's for sure. He needed me and so did the class if this play was going to be good.

"Great," said Mr. Cowles, "then let's get started. I have chosen your parts for you, so that everyone gets a chance to speak."

I frowned and shook my head. Should I tell him? Of course I should. He can't help it if he doesn't know anything about real theatre. Up went my hand again.

Mr. Cowles tilted his head to one side like he was thinking about something, then he nodded at me slowly.

"When I tried out for *Joseph*, Director Nielson said he picked each one of us *very carefully*. Shouldn't a *real* play have tryouts?"

"Yeah!" called out Sabrina and Roberta.

"Tryouts! Tryouts! Tryouts!" the class chanted.

Mr. Cowles waved his hands to quiet everyone down. Then he squeezed his eyebrows together again and his lips grew smaller. "Mmm . . . I didn't want to spend a lot of class time on this . . . I want to put it on in two weeks."

Two weeks! That didn't give me much time to help them. "That's okay," I shouted. "We can have the tryouts at recess. I know how they work. Let me, Mr. Cowles."

"Yeah, let Ashley. We want a *real* play," Sabrina pleaded.

"Please, Mr. Cowles, please?" begged the girls sitting around me. They all thought I was even better at this than Mr. Cowles. Being in a play was the best thing that ever happened to me.

"Okay, okay, if that's the way you want it."

"Yeah!" everyone exclaimed.

I hugged myself. Wow! Now I was in charge!

Mr. Cowles glanced up at the big white clock on the wall and gasped, "My goodness! It's nearly time for recess already! Take out your spelling lists, class. You can practice your spelling words with your partners until the bell."

Everyone started whispering and dragging their chairs over to their partners. I could hear they were whispering about our play.

Krystal was my partner. She was a good speller. She never missed a letter. She always said she could see the words in her head. Not me though. I have to practise and practise. But I couldn't think of spelling today. All I could think of was our class play and recess.

Krystal pulled her chair up beside mine and we hid our faces behind her spelling book.

"You know sooo much about plays already," Krystal whispered to me. "And we shouldn't practise when you are away."

I stared at her. "I'm not going anywhere."

"Yes you are," Krystal giggled. "Remember . . . one afternoon a week. You told me last night on the phone you get one afternoon off a week from school to practise *Joseph*, and the rest of the practices are at night."

"Oh yeah!" I giggled too. "I'm going to learn everything I can in my *really* real play and teach everyone here. And just wait till you see the auditions!"

Krystal nodded her head hard. "Ashley, you'll make everything great. Only . . . " Krystal chewed on her fingernail and her cheeks got redder.

"Only what?"

"What are . . . aw-dish-uns?" Krystal asked.

I smiled and leaned forward. "Bring out your pencil and a piece of paper at recess. You can be my assistant and I'll show you exactly what to do!"

# Chapter 3

# The Great Aw-dish-uns

"Tryouts are *really* called auditions . . . and they're very important," I explained outside on the playground. Lots of kids smiled and stuck out their chests. We all stood on the grass beside the blacktop. Close enough to the tetherball stand for the crowd there to hear us.

I told everyone from my class to get into a long line. Some of the grade ones and twos drifted over to see what was going on. Even the teacher on duty stopped to watch.

"Come on, Clayton! We don't want to be in any wimpy play. You're supposed to be goalie!" yelled Jason and Sean, the pesky twins who sit at the back of my room.

Clayton eyed me and dug the toe of his shoe into the grass. He was the first in line. "I'll just be a minute," he called back.

The boys shrugged and ran away. I grinned.

"What part are you trying out for?" I asked in a low voice, trying to sound like Director Nielson. Krystal looked at me and giggled.

"Shhhh," I warned her. "This is supposed to be very serious."

"Oh!" She nodded, and frowned at Clayton.

"I want to be the Scarecrow," Clayton announced.

I sat down on the grass with Krystal beside me. She was my assistant now.

"Write down his name and put Scarecrow beside it," I told Krystal. She nodded and printed the words on her paper.

"What are you going to do for us today?" I

asked in my low, director's voice.

Clayton stared at us blankly. "What?"

I sighed. "You're supposed to do something. You know . . . pretend you're in a movie, sing a song, anything, so I can see how good you are."

All the kids in line started whispering.

"Silence!" I roared. "I will not take any interruptions in my rehearsal hall!" I was very pleased. I sounded just like Director Nielson. The first time he yelled at us, I nearly peed my pants. Everyone in the line stood still, no one said a word, even the grass didn't move.

"But we're outside on the playground!" Krystal whispered to me.

"I know that!" I snapped at her. "But we have to pretend."

Krystal glared at me for a second and then she looked down at her paper. Her cheeks were red.

Some more little kids showed up and even some of the kids in the older grades. The tetherball was left dangling. Now I had a crowd. It was getting exciting.

Clayton stuffed his hands into his pockets and made a face. "I'm not singing any stupid song. I just want to be the Scarecrow!"

"Why?" I demanded.

"Because I like the Scarecrow best."

I nodded. "Write that down," I whispered to Krystal.

She bobbed her head and busily started to print again.

Clayton glared at me and growled. I looked him up and down. Clayton would be a perfect Scarecrow, he was so skinny and wobbly. His hair even looked like straw. But I would never tell him. That was not how it was done.

"Well, you have to do something, or you can't have the part. It's the rules. Show me how the Scarecrow acts."

Clayton sighed and threw his arms up in the air. He took a step towards us and suddenly one of his knees seemed to crumble. He nearly hit the ground, but just as quick as he went down he was back up again. He walked around in a circle like his bones were made of Jell-O.

Everyone started laughing and clapping. Then he made made silly faces and wriggled around as though he had bugs in his pants. His audience laughed harder. The duty teacher laughed the loudest.

"You're a natural, Clayton!" she called out in her squeaky voice, then she moved on.

Krystal dropped her papers and started clapping too.

"Stop that!" I hissed at her. "He's not supposed to know he's good."

"Oh!" She scrambled up her papers and pretended to print.

"That's fine, Clayton Pratt, you may go now. I've seen enough."

Clayton put his hands on his hips. "Do I get the part or not?"

"Maybe. You'll find out when I put up the list."

"What?" he yelled.

"Goodbye."

Clayton kicked at the grass and stomped away.

I smiled. This was the first time I had ever ordered Clayton Pratt away, and he actually left. Being the director was almost better than being in the play.

Krystal looked at me and smiled. "You're a good boss," she whispered.

"Director," I corrected her. "Next."

# Chapter 4

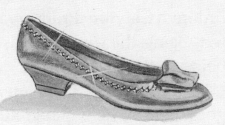

# Who's the Best?

Julia stepped forward. "I want to be Dorothy," she announced, kicking up her feet and whirling around. "I want to wear ruby slippers and melt the Wicked Witch." Her voice sounded gushy and sweet. I wrinkled my nose.

"But I want to be Dorothy!" yelled Sarah, who was after Julia.

"So do I!" added Sarah's best friend Roberta.

"Well, you can't all be Dorothy," I hollered at them. They got quiet. Sarah looked like she was going to cry.

"Uh, Ashley . . . " It was Krystal.

"What now?"

"Recess is nearly over."

"Oh, rats." I tugged on my hair to help me think. Then I remembered. "Okay, everyone who wants to be Dorothy, stand in a circle around me."

Almost every girl there scrambled into a big ring. Krystal had to push her way through to get beside me. She didn't have her assistant's papers. I figured she wanted to be Dorothy too.

"I am going to show you how Dorothy acts in the play and all of you do what I do." I clasped my hands together and pretended to cry.

"Oh, Auntie Em," I whimpered. "Where are you? Where are you?" I'd seen it a million times at Krystal's.

I looked around the circle. "Well, what are

you waiting for? Go ahead and try it!" I hollered.

The girls nervously clasped their hands together and all started wailing. They sounded like screeching crows.

"No. No. No. No." I wiggled my finger at each of them. "You have to make me *believe* you!" I bellowed in my best Director Nielson voice.

All of the girls looked around at each other and shrugged.

"Maybe you should show us again," suggested Sabrina.

I fell on my knees. "Auntie Em! Oh, Auntie Em, I miss you so!"

I got up. "Like that."

They got down on their knees and moaned, only louder.

"Yuck!" I said. "I can't *feel* it!"

They glanced around and rose to their feet. Julia's shoulders sagged. Sarah looked like she was going to cry again.

I sighed. I was saying just what Director

Nielson said at his auditions. But here at school they just didn't get it.

"Ashley," said Sabrina. "I don't think anyone can do it as well as you. After all, you're in *Joseph*."

"That's true," I answered her.

"Maybe *you* should be Dorothy."

"Yeah," Sarah and Roberta agreed.

I smiled. I could see me on the stage in the gym with the whole school clapping for me. I would be the school star.

"But Krystal looks like Dorothy. Maybe Krystal should be Dorothy," added Julia.

I looked at Krystal. She did look like Dorothy. Her long black hair hung in two neat braids. She was even wearing a dress like Dorothy's. And I knew she could sing.

Krystal's eyes got wide while I looked at her. Her cheeks puffed out. She was holding her breath. She looked excited. She looked hopeful.

I frowned. Krystal was good, but she couldn't be as good as me. And this show had to be the best. I turned away and faced Sabrina. "You're right, Sabrina. I'm the one who should do it. I'm going to be Dorothy. After all, I'm in *Joseph*."

Just then the bell went and everyone started running towards the door. I ran faster than anyone. I felt funny about facing Krystal. But she'd understand . . . wouldn't she?

# Chapter 5

# I'll Show You How

"Last night, at my rehearsal . . . " I smiled and looked at the girls sitting on the carpet right in front of me. Everyone leaned forward. I didn't have to bring anything for Sharing Time any more. I just had to stand up. "Brandon Colt spoke to me."

"The *real* Brandon Colt?"

"Wow."

"He's so cute!"

"Can I have his autograph?"

"Girls!" Mr. Cowles broke in. "Please raise your hands." I loved it when they forgot to put up their hands. It meant they were excited.

It was the same way at auditions yesterday. Things went really well. Kids crowded around all through morning recess, lunch and afternoon recess. Now everyone in the school knew my name. The principal even congratulated me during morning announcements!

Sabrina raised her hand. I pointed to her.

"So what did Brandon Colt say?"

Say? Hmm. I looked at all of the faces looking up at me. "He told me . . . I was great."

"Really?"

"Wow."

They all started talking at once again. Krystal just stared at me. I wondered what I would tell them tomorrow.

When I sat down, Krystal leaned in and whispered, "You told me he said that to everyone in the choir."

I knotted my hands together and turned to her

slowly. "So?" I whispered back. "It's the same thing. I'm in the choir, aren't I? So, he was talking to me." I glared at her, making my eyes big.

Krystal's eyes narrowed into little slits. She pushed her lips together until they turned white, but she didn't say anything. I looked down at the carpet. How would I get myself out of this one?

"Krystal," I whispered, leaning closer but not looking at her. "You're going to be a great Munchkin, but I think you can handle a bigger role. That's why, if I get sick, I want you to be Dorothy." I faced her. "Will you be my understudy?"

Krystal stopped looking mad. She sort of smiled. Then she nodded. I smiled a little, too, but my stomach felt funny, like I hadn't done something nice at all.

☆　☆　☆

After lunch Mr. Cowles told us it was time to start practising our play.

"Rehearsing," I corrected him. He nodded but he didn't smile.

He marched us down to the gym in a long line. He had the paper with my list on a clipboard. It made my list look important. My name was at the top as Dorothy. He had a script for everyone too. It felt almost like a real play.

"Let's start at the beginning of the play." He passed out the scripts. We all sat in a wide circle on the hard floor.

Clayton Pratt was going to be the Scarecrow. Sabrina was the Good Witch and Sarah was the Wicked Witch. Jason and Sean and some of the other boys agreed to be the Wicked Witch's Flying Monkeys. But only if they could be mean. They wanted to eat up Toto, Dorothy's dog, but I said no. Even if it was only a stuffed toy, that was too mean. But I agreed to talk to Mr. Cowles about letting them be a little nasty.

Most of the kids were Munchkins.

"Dorothy, Auntie Em, Toto and Uncle Henry can go and stand up on the stage," Mr. Cowles announced.

"*No!*" I blurted out.

Everyone looked at me.

"What's the matter?" demanded Mr. Cowles. He did not look pleased.

"Mr. Cowles, we have to warm up our voices first."

Some of the kids started to giggle.

Mr. Cowles shifted his clipboard from one hand to the other. He pushed his glasses down to the end of his nose.

"Ashley. This is not a play like *Joseph*. We don't need to do every — "

"But you don't understand! Director Nielson said that *all* plays, even school plays, must take care of the actors. He said he's met lots of kids who have no voices left because some dumb director wasn't careful."

Some of the kids gasped. I wasn't sure why at first. Then I thought about what I had just said. I swallowed and looked down at my shoes.

I really didn't mean that Mr. Cowles was dumb!

There wasn't a sound in the gym except for the hum of the big lights. Then I heard someone giggle. It sounded just like Clayton. My head shot up.

"Honest, Mr. Cowles, Director Nielson said that. It's dangerous not to warm up."

Mr. Cowles hugged the clipboard to his chest and looked around at everyone sitting on the tile floor. Some of the girls were holding their throats. Maybe they thought their voices would suddenly pop out and fly away. Mr. Cowles slowly nodded his head.

"Okay, Ashley. Perhaps you should show us how to warm up our voices."

I grinned. "Stand up, everyone."

Slowly they all got to their feet. Mr. Cowles walked over to the wall and leaned against it.

"Open up your mouths real wide. Wider. Stretch it. Now close it." We did that again and again. "Now pretend you're chewing gum."

"What's this got to do with our voices?" Clayton whined.

"Now, say ahhhhhhhh. Now hum," I

instructed. Some of the kids began to wriggle around and make faces at each other.

"That's enough!" I yelled.

They were all quiet again.

Mr. Cowles walked over to us. "You did that very well, Ashley," he said calmly.

"Thank you," I smiled. I was sure I'd done it better than he could.

Then one of the big gym doors swung open and the librarian, Mrs. Benny, hurried in.

She was always in a hurry. She reminded me of a chicken. A fussy chicken. Her frilly white blouse fluttered and her high shoes clicked across the gym floor. She stopped and wiggled her finger at Mr. Cowles so he would come over to her. She talked in a hush. But I could tell she was worked up about something.

I sighed and glanced over at Krystal. She looked to the ceiling and sighed too. "Now what?" I muttered. Mrs. Benny never had good news.

# Chapter 6

# Taking Control

"Now?" Mr. Cowles' voice rang out over our heads.

Mrs. Benny's head bounced around on her neck. Her voice raced on.

"How many days?" Mr. Cowles said even more loudly. He shook his head from side to side and slowly walked back to us.

"Grade threes, I have to attend a meeting this morning ... and most mornings this week.

No *Wizard of Oz* today, I'm afraid. Mrs. Benny will take you back to class."

"But what about our rehearsal?" I moaned.

"Our voices are all ready," Sabrina whined.

"A play?" Mrs. Benny cooed. "Oh, what fun. When I taught kindergarten, we put on lots of little plays." She beamed at us. We all looked at each other nervously.

"But I must admit, I've never directed anything as ambitious as *The Wizard of Oz*!" Her voice went up so high I thought the lights might crack. "I should go get my pitch pipe!"

Mrs. Benny our director? A kindergarten play? What was a pitch pipe?

I gulped loudly. She'll have the Wicked Witch blowing kisses and the ugly Monkeys wearing pretty bows. Oh no! I closed my eyes. The play was ruined.

I could hear the twins grumbling and shuffling close by. They'd quit the play for sure now. Some of girls sighed loudly.

Mr. Cowles cleared his throat. "Hah-hum." Everything was quiet. Only the lights hummed.

"Thank you, Mrs. Benny, I do need you to supervise . . . " he said, his voice trailing off, "but I think we have a director."

I squinted my eyes open and looked sideways at Krystal. She squinted back. She raised up her shoulders and let them drop down. What was he talking about?

I looked up at him. Mr. Cowles looked right back at me.

"Ashley Lawrence will be directing," he said. "She knows a lot about plays." He pushed his clipboard out towards me.

I stopped breathing. My hands reached out slowly and grasped the end of his clipboard. My eyes got wider and wider. Mr. Cowles leaned forward. "Have a good . . . *rehearsal*," he said slowly. Then he turned and walked to the door.

I grabbed my script off the floor and laid it on top of my new director's clipboard.

"Auntie Em, Uncle Henry, Toto, Dorothy, on stage!" I bellowed.

"But you're Dorothy! You can't be the

director and Dorothy at the same time!" Clayton shouted.

"I can too. Krystal is Dorothy during rehearsal. She's my understudy."

Krystal gasped and snatched up her script. She ran for the stage. The other students in the first act ran too.

"The rest of you sit on the floor at the bottom of the stage."

They stood around, not quite sure whether to listen to me.

"NOW!" I screamed. They took off like a flock of wild geese.

"Oh my!" I heard Mrs. Benny say.

I glanced behind me. Mr. Cowles was standing in the doorway, watching. He just stood there for a few seconds, staring. His mouth dropped open like he was going to say something, but no words came out. His fingers drummed on the doorframe. It was like he didn't know whether or not to leave. Oh, no. Was he going to change his mind? Then he suddenly gave me a thumbs-up and walked out the door. It closed with a thud behind him.

I hugged my clipboard. Then I turned and watched everyone scurry into place. This play was going to be fantastic. And now, it was all mine!

# Chapter 7

# Setting the Stage

"Go upstage!" I repeated. Clayton looked around. Everyone onstage shook their heads. Nobody knew where upstage was.

"That way, that way!" I pointed to the back of the stage and sighed.

"Why don't you just use normal words?" Clayton demanded.

"Because then it isn't a *real* play, is it?" I had to learn all this stuff in *Joseph*. Now they had to learn it too. I was going to be as good a director as Director Nielson.

"You'll catch on," I said to Clayton and rolled my eyes just like Director Nielson did to me. Then I flopped down in my director's chair. I had placed it right in the middle of the gym, so I could see the whole stage and the kids sitting on the floor waiting for their turn.

Clayton skulked off to the corner. He kicked at the stage floor with his runners. It made a *squeak, squeak* noise. I sighed again, loudly. So he could hear me.

We rehearsed almost for an hour. A lot longer than I thought we would get to. Mrs. Benny never interfered, not even once. I told everyone on stage where to go and explained that was called "blocking." And I also told them they couldn't change where I put them.

Plus, I corrected everything they did wrong. I was amazed at how much I noticed from sitting in my director's chair.

"Sabrina!" I ordered, "don't whisper to someone else onstage."

"Clayton, get your finger out of your nose!"

"Julia! Don't play with your hair while the Good Witch is talking!"

"Clayton, stop cleaning your ears!"

"Sarah, speak louder!"

"Clayton, stop tugging at your wedgie!"

By the end of the rehearsal, most of the girls were afraid to move, which was just fine.

"Less fidgeting, more focus!" I yelled, just like Director Nielson.

My only disappointment was Clayton. Every time I told him what he was doing wrong, he got less and less funny. Now, he still fidgeted, but didn't wobble or act silly. Oh, well. He would get funny again before the play went on. That's how Director Nielson did it.

When Mrs. Benny called everyone off the stage I told them to get into a big semicircle around my director's chair.

"Whatever for?" asked Mrs. Benny. "It's time to go back to class."

"We haven't had 'notes' yet," I exclaimed.

"Oh, of course," she muttered and backed away. Her head jiggled around on her neck like it was loose.

"Notes," I explained to everyone, "is when the director tells you how the rehearsal went." I noticed Mrs. Benny was listening too.

Everyone leaned closer. Some nodded and whispered.

I tapped my pencil on the edge of my clipboard. Then I rubbed my chin. A hush fell over the class. "This," I said shaking my head, "was a bad rehearsal."

No one spoke. They looked disappointed.

"You will need a lot of work. Especially the Munchkins," I added.

There was a shuffling sound. One of the Munchkins coughed.

"You didn't look like you knew what you were doing!" I pointed out.

The boys snickered.

I turned to them. "And you Flying Monkeys . . . "

The boys went silent.

"You need to concentrate. You didn't look scary at all."

Some of the Munchkins stuck out their tongues at the Monkeys. Some of the Monkeys made cross-eyes at the Munchkins. Mrs. Benny clucked her tongue.

I thought for a minute. Was there anything else I was supposed to say? Oh, yes.

"Try harder tomorrow. Dismissed."

"Wow," said Krystal as we got ready to leave the gym. "You really know what you're doing."

I smiled my best smile.

Some of the girls crowded around. "You made it so . . . so . . . " Sabrina didn't seem to know how to say it.

"Real," I finished for her.

"Right. I'm going to ask my mother to come and see this."

"Me too," they all agreed.

"I'm going to invite my father," Krystal announced.

My smile faded. Poor Krystal. She really

missed her dad. I wished for her that he would come, but I didn't think he would. He called and called her and said he'd visit. But Krystal hadn't seen him in a month.

Mrs. Benny stepped into our group.

"Don't you think this is a little too serious for a class play?" she asked looking from one girl to the other. Finally, her crinkled eyes stared right at me.

"But Ashley is showing us the right way," insisted Krystal. The others bobbed their heads up and down.

"We want it to be just like *Joseph*," Sabrina said defiantly.

"Oh." Mrs. Benny was still for a moment. Then she added, "We always had lots of fun when I did plays with my classes."

No one said anything for a few seconds. They fidgeted around. None of them looked at me.

I sniffed. Kindergarten plays! "Plays are serious business," I answered Mrs. Benny in my best director's voice. Her eyebrows shot

up but she didn't say anything more.

I would show what being in a real play meant. I would show them all.

# Chapter 8

# Taking It

I could feel Krystal watching me as I flipped my special *Joseph* eraser back and forth across my desk.

I felt like dropping it on the floor and stepping on it. Last night Director Nielson screamed at me for waving the wrong hand at the end of a song. I kept hearing his voice inside my head, yelling out my name in front of everyone. My stomach felt like a hard candy with a tight wrapper.

"Directors are mean," I suddenly blurted out.

Krystal looked surprised. "I thought they were supposed to be mean."

I bit my lip. Could I tell her I hated Director Nielson? That I didn't want to go back to my *Joseph* rehearsal? What if she told the other kids in the class?

"They *are* supposed to be mean," I answered her. "The Costume Mistress says Director Nielson is demanding and that makes him the best. She told the children's choir that if we want to be in a real play we have to be able to take it." I swallowed hard. I would take it.

"Don't you ever have any fun at all?" Krystal asked quietly.

I thought for a second, then I shook my head. "Not supposed to," I announced, pressing my eraser hard against my desk.

"Oh," she said. She sounded sad.

The wrapper around my stomach squeezed tighter. I wished I could tell her the truth.

Suddenly Krystal sighed and said, "Au-di-tion."

I looked at her for a second, then I remembered. Oh yeah, spelling. "A," I said back to her. She nodded her head yes.

"U, D . . . "

Krystal nodded some more.

I bit at my bottom lip. "I . . . S?"

We had picked our special spelling words this week to go with our class play. I was beginning to wish we hadn't. I knew how to run auditions, but I sure couldn't spell them.

Krystal could, though. "T," she corrected me. Krystal knew our script backwards and forwards, too. When anyone got stuck on their lines, she could tell them what to say. Krystal was almost as good at plays as I was.

We'd been rehearsing all week and everything was going great. Mrs. Benny tried to help sometimes, squawking and flapping as always. But she kept using the wrong words. When I told her the right words she would get really quiet, and her eyes would get round, like she was laying an egg. It was funny.

When Mr. Cowles finished his meetings, he let me stay the director. He said he was the producer now, whatever that was. Mom told me the producer is the person with all the money. I was surprised because I didn't think Mr. Cowles was rich.

Suddenly the school secretary's voice boomed over the P.A.

"Would Ashley Lawrence please come to the office?"

"Ooh, woo," teased Clayton. Some of the other boys joined in. Clayton gave one of the twins a high five.

I made a face at him. I knew I wasn't in trouble. My mother was supposed to pick me up this morning before lunch. I had my first fitting for my costume for *Joseph*.

"Say hi to Brandon Colt," sang out Sabrina.

"Bye, Ashley!" called out most of the girls. They all looked so happy for me. But Krystal just looked me in the eye and whispered, "Good luck."

☆ ☆ ☆

The fitting went way late. Everyone in the costume room for *Joseph* was crabby and bossy. I squirmed and squirmed. The blouse to my costume was too tight. The skirt was itchy. And it was orange. I hate the colour orange. I complained to the Costume Mistress and she complained about me to Director Nielson.

When we had to stand on stage for the Costume Designer and Director Nielson to look at us I yelped. The dumb Costume Mistress left a pin in my skirt that jabbed me. But she didn't get hollered at — I did. I wanted to cry.

It all took so long my mom didn't even have time to take me out for lunch like she'd promised. She had to get back to work.

In the car my mom told me I didn't look very happy about my rehearsal. "You don't have to be in *Joseph*," she said. She handed me some warm cheese and a spotted banana to eat. "You can quit if you're not enjoying yourself."

"Quit?" I couldn't do that. No one would listen to me any more. I couldn't direct the class play. Maybe *Joseph* was no fun at all. But I couldn't quit. I just couldn't.

"No," I answered her. "Everything is fine." I pushed my back up against the seat and stared out the window. I squashed the cheese into a lumpy orange ball.

# Chapter 9

# Second Best

When I finally got back to my classroom, nobody was there.

"Where the heck are you?" I yelled over the empty desks. Then suddenly, I knew.

I stomped down the hall. My footsteps sounded like a giant's. Even before I reached the gym I could hear them. But they were laughing. Nobody ever laughed in my rehearsals. I wouldn't allow it.

I clenched my teeth together. They weren't supposed to practise when I wasn't at school. I gripped the door handle and was just about to pull it open when I heard Mr. Cowles say my name. I stopped dead and listened.

"But that was fantastic," he was saying. Then I heard clapping. "I'll tell Ashley to do it *your* way. It was delightful!"

Then I heard the kids in the class yelling, "Do it again! Do it again!"

Who were they cheering for? My hand tightened on the handle. Who was doing better than me? I pulled open the door just a crack and peered through the opening. Most of the class was on the stage. Standing in the middle was Krystal. Her cheeks were so pink she looked like she was on fire.

Krystal? I pressed my teeth together harder.

"No, no, let's move on . . . ," Mr. Cowles was saying. "Start the song, Krystal."

I held my breath and pulled open the door a little wider.

All the kids got quiet when Krystal opened

her mouth. She stepped forward and reached out with her arms like she was about to hug the world. Her voice rang out through the big room, filling it up with music. She looked like she was glowing. My stomach almost flipped over.

Instead of standing still like I always did, she strolled across the stage, singing and singing. Then she leaned against the side wall of the stage, beside the big curtain. She gazed up like she was searching for a rainbow. She looked as though she were floating on a soft cloud.

Who told you to do that? I wanted to scream. A big rock formed in my stomach, weighing me down.

Every one of the kids in the class stared at her like she was magic. I looked at Mr. Cowles. He had the biggest smile on his face I'd ever seen. He never looked like that when I sang.

I yanked open the door as hard as I could and pulled it shut behind me. The dull thud echoed through the gym.

Krystal looked towards the door and then right at me. I jabbed my fists into my hips and glared at her hard.

The sound of her singing slowly died away.

# Chapter 10

# Being a REAL Director

An empty silence filled the room.

Mr. Cowles turned around. "Oh, hello, Ashley. We were just — "

"Rehearsing," I cut in.

"Well . . . yes." Mr. Cowles frowned at me.

I jabbed my finger at the kids onstage. "*They* were not following *my* blocking!" The kids sitting on the floor twisted around to see me.

Mr. Cowles' eyes got wider and his mouth

dropped open, but no words came out. I could feel everyone staring at me. I thought my face would burn up.

"Clayton!" I screamed. "You were pulling at your pants again! Get your mother to buy you boxers before the next rehearsal!"

"Ashley!" I heard Mr. Cowles exclaim. I ignored him.

"Sabrina! You forgot a line *again*. By now you should know the script! Go home and practise or else."

I felt Mr. Cowles move up beside me.

"And Krystal!" I glared at her. My voice kept getting louder and louder. "You didn't do ANYTHING right!"

Krystal clasped her hands together. She looked like she was shrinking, standing up there on the stage. No one moved.

"Ashley Lawrence!" shouted Mr. Cowles. "That is quite enough!"

I turned and looked at him. His face was as white as chalk. His eyes looked like flickering candles. I had seen Mr. Cowles angry before, but not like this. It was the first time he had ever yelled at anyone in our class. And he was yelling at me.

Everyone was deathly still. They all stared at me. I felt like a bug on the sidewalk about to be squashed.

"Ashley, I am removing you as Director," Mr. Cowles said. His voice was cold. My stomach squeezed tight. My eyes stung. Someone on stage clapped. I felt like I was going to cry. I gritted my teeth. I looked down at the floor to hide my face.

"Mr. Cowles."

I looked up.

It was Krystal. She walked to the edge of the stage and stood quietly.

"What Ashley said is true. I wasn't following my directions." Then she looked right at me. Her eyes looked sad and hard at the same time. "Ashley is only being the *best* director. I can take it."

My eyes blurred and I couldn't see her any more. Best director? Me? And then I understood. I was just like Director Nielson.

# Chapter 11

# Sharing

"Sharing Time!" Mr. Cowles announced first thing Monday morning. Everyone scrambled for the carpet.

Sabrina sat down first. Julia and Roberta sat on one side of her. Sabrina grabbed Krystal's hand and pulled her down on the other side. I stood behind them. Their backs looked like a wall. I plopped down on the carpet by myself.

It was Clayton's turn to share first. He kept his Sharing hidden in his hands.

"Is it a toy?"

Clayton shook his head.

"Is it alive?"

Clayton wiggled his eyebrows and shook his head hard. An excited buzz filled the room. I said nothing. The kids used to be excited like that when I got up to share. Now I wasn't so sure they still would be.

While everyone watched Clayton, Sabrina passed a sticky worm candy to Julia and Roberta. Sabrina jerked her head around and looked at me. She just stared for a second. Then she turned away. No sticky worms for me.

Then she offered a sticky worm to Krystal. Krystal shook her head. I waited for her to look back at me, but she didn't.

I'd thought about Krystal all weekend, but I hadn't called. I missed her.

Clayton uncovered his Sharing. It was a fake eyeball frozen into a pretend ice cube.

"You put it in someone's drink!" Clayton declared.

The twins hooted. Sabrina and Sarah shrieked. Everyone else laughed.

The laughter echoed in my ears. I pulled at my spiral shoelaces. *Sprong. Sprong. Sprong.* I counted the holes the laces wound through.

A strange feeling crept up my spine. I glanced up. Everyone was staring at me.

"I said," Mr. Cowles' voice boomed from behind me, "it's your turn, Ashley."

Sabrina and Sarah giggled.

"I . . . don't have . . . anything," I croaked.

"You know the rules, Ashley. Share a thing, a happening or a thought."

I nodded and licked my lips. Slowly, I stood up. I faced the class. The kids on the floor rustled around. Sabrina and Julia whispered to each other. I just stood there. I felt like Clayton's eyeball, frozen onto the spot.

"Why don't you tell us about *Joseph*?" prompted Mr. Cowles.

Clayton moaned out loud. "Aww! Do we have to hear about that stupid play *again*?"

No one wanted to hear about *Joseph* any more. My throat felt dry.

"Clayton, raise your hand if you have

something to say," Mr. Cowles warned him. I pressed my lips together. He didn't get mad at Clayton for saying my play was stupid. Mr. Cowles didn't like me any more, either. My hands felt cold.

"Did you have a rehearsal on the weekend?" asked Mr. Cowles.

I nodded.

"Well? . . . "

I looked out the window. Three big black crows perched on the telephone wires. They were staring at me too.

"Ashley?"

I looked at Mr. Cowles and sighed. "Yesterday, at my rehearsal . . . "

Sabrina passed another sticky worm to Julia. Krystal kept her head down. I couldn't see her face.

"Brandon Colt . . . " I continued, "he told me . . . "

Krystal raised her head and looked right at me. Her lips were pressed together so tight they looked wrinkled.

I swallowed.

"Brandon Colt said to me . . . "

Krystal's eyes narrowed.

I knew what I had to say. But could I do it? I drew in a quick breath. "I mean . . . Brandon Colt said to us . . . everyone in the children's choir . . . "

Krystal's eyes widened.

"He said we needed more rehearsal time, so we had another rehearsal last night."

The rustling noise from the carpet stopped. Krystal stopped wrinkling her lips.

"Did it help?" Julia asked.

I shook my head. "While I was onstage, Director Nielson yelled at me for pulling on my shirt." My throat felt tight. I looked at Krystal. My voice got quiet. "I . . . I started to . . . I had to leave the rehearsal and go home."

Clayton nudged the kid beside him and they snickered. Julia and Roberta looked at each other and then back at me. Sabrina rolled her eyes, just like Director Nielson. Krystal stared. Her mouth had dropped open. She looked surprised at first, and then her eyes drooped like she had a pain. I couldn't look up at Mr. Cowles. I was quiet for a long time and nobody asked me any more questions.

"Thank you, Ashley," said Mr. Cowles. "You may sit down now."

Sharing was over. After Sharing we were having another play practice . . . I mean rehearsal. I wished I could just go home. I didn't want to have another rehearsal. I was sick of rehearsals.

I waited till the line had nearly left the classroom. Then I joined on. I dragged my feet all the way down the hall. *Swish. Swish. Swish.* When I was just about to go into the gym, Mr. Cowles tapped me on the shoulder.

"Ashley, could I speak to you privately, please?"

I nodded and gulped. Mr. Cowles poked his head inside the door to give some instructions to the class. Then he let the big door swing shut. We stood alone in the empty hall. Wasn't I going to be allowed in the play at all? I twisted my fingers into the bottom of my sweat shirt.

I looked up. Mr. Cowles was looking down at me. He was not smiling, but he did not look mad either.

"Ashley . . . I've been thinking about what happened at play rehearsal on Friday." Mr. Cowles' voice was calm.

I wriggled around and stared at my shoes.

"I think you should still be our director."

I held very still. Did I hear him right?

"I feel it was my fault that you yelled at the other students. Being a director is a big responsibility. I should have helped you more . . . " His voice trailed off.

I looked at him. His eyes looked so sad. It was Mr. Cowles' fault? No, that wasn't right. It was my fault! But I didn't know what to say.

"Ashley, I would like you to try again. But this time I want you to be kinder to your classmates. Think of their feelings."

I nodded. My neck felt stiff.

"You need to help them," he added.

I looked past him. Help them? How do I do that? I wondered.

"Clayton, for instance, is nervous about performing in front of grown-ups."

"Clayton?" I blurted out.

"Yes," Mr. Cowles assured me. "He needs some encouragement. I think you are the one to give it to him."

I couldn't believe what Mr. Cowles was saying. Me help Clayton?

"But h-how?" I managed to stammer.

Now Mr. Cowles smiled. "I'm sure you'll think of a way."

He pulled open the big door and invited me to go inside. I stepped into the gym. The class was standing in a circle warming up their voices, just the way I had taught them to. I wanted to swallow, but I couldn't. This was my second chance, and I didn't have a clue what to do.

# Chapter 12

# Am I Doing This Right?

I stood and watched. I felt hot all over. Did the caretaker turn up the heat in here?

When they were finished, Mr. Cowles nodded at me. "Th . . . that was good," I said quietly. The kids glanced around at each other.

"You can't — " It was Clayton, but Mr. Cowles cut him off.

"Ashley will remain our director, after all," said Mr. Cowles.

Some of the kids groaned. Clayton groaned the loudest. I didn't hear anything from Krystal. My stomach felt as though it had a hole in it.

"That's enough!" Mr. Cowles warned them and he clapped his hands together. "Ashley is learning, just like you. We will start where we left off on Friday. So get into your positions. Only three more days, remember. The play goes on Thursday!"

The class got into their positions on stage. Krystal stood in the middle as my understudy. Mr. Cowles brought over two chairs and we both sat down.

"Action," I called in a crackly voice. I sat down. The rehearsal began.

Sabrina missed two lines, Clayton pulled at his pants and the Munchkins kept bumping into each other. The Flying Monkeys were the worst ever. They looked like dodo birds. Big, goofy dodo birds.

I remembered how Director Nielson had yelled at me when I'd used the wrong hand. I hadn't done it on purpose. The Munchkins couldn't be bumping into each other on purpose. The Flying Monkeys didn't want to look like dodo birds.

I sat swinging my legs under my chair until Mr. Cowles announced it was time to end the rehearsal.

Everyone filed off the stage and sat down in their semicircle in front of me. They knew they had made mistakes. I could tell by their faces.

My mouth felt dry. I licked my lips and stood up. Everyone stared. What should I do? Suddenly I brought my hands together hard. *Smack. Smack. Smack.* The noise sounded hollow in the big gym. Everyone looked at everyone else.

"Good rehearsal," I announced and I sat down.

"But I forgot a line," Sabrina said out loud.

I shrugged. "You'll remember tomorrow," I said.

Sabrina smiled.

"Julia stepped on my foot!" called out Roberta.

I nodded again. "Yes, I noticed, but it was sort of funny. Do it again tomorrow, Julia."

Julia giggled and so did some of the other girls.

"What about us?" asked the twins.

"Uh, I liked the growling. Monkeys should growl even more." All at once the Monkeys started to growl. Then, one of the boys barked. Soon they were all barking. Everyone started to laugh. Barking Monkeys. It was silly, but I laughed too. It felt good to laugh.

Now everyone was smiling and looking more relaxed. Maybe plays could be fun after all. I looked over at Krystal. She was smiling the widest smile of all.

I spotted Clayton. He was not smiling. His shoulders still sagged. How could I help him? Then I remembered. There was one thing Director Nielson said to the grownups in the play when they were really good. It was special. A *real play* thing to say.

I cleared my throat and stood up. I looked right at Clayton.

"Clayton," I said loudly. He squinted at me.

"Clayton, I'm sure during our play . . . " I paused. "You will be the one to *break a leg!*" I beamed at him.

Clayton's eyes got smaller and his cheeks turned red. A small titter started at one end of the semicircle and grew until everyone sitting on the floor was laughing and laughing. I looked around. What were they laughing at?

Clayton stood up.

"Break a leg, eh?" he snarled at me. "Well, I hope you break your neck!" He took a step towards me and swung his fist at my head.

"Hey, hey, hey!" Mr. Cowles stepped between us, just in time. He caught Clayton by the shoulders and bent over to talk to him.

I flopped down in my chair. I had blown it again.

"Clayton. You know better than that!" Mr. Cowles scolded him.

Clayton looked down at the floor.

"I'm tired of her making fun of me." Clayton's voice was shaking.

I had never seen Clayton so miserable. But I was not happy about it. I felt crummy. Mr. Cowles was counting on me to help Clayton and I made things worse.

"You need to understand what Director Ashley was saying to you," Mr. Cowles went on. "She was paying you a compliment."

"Yeah, right," said Clayton. "She said I was clumsy."

"No, no. Ashley, please explain."

I looked up at Mr. Cowles. He looked hopeful. Maybe he wasn't mad at me. He certainly understood I was trying to help.

I got out of my chair and stepped towards them, but not too close, just in case Clayton didn't like my compliment.

" 'Break a leg' means . . . be the best."

Clayton glanced over at Mr. Cowles. He looked doubtful.

"Honest," I insisted. "You'll break a leg

because you're the funniest thing in the play. That's why I picked you to be the Scarecrow."

"Really?" Clayton whispered.

"Heck, yeah. I could tell when you auditioned you'd be great." I smiled at him.

A big grin spread over Clayton's face. It was the first time he had ever smiled at me.

Suddenly, the twins started to clap.

Clayton made a big bow. He walked around in his wobbly Scarecrow way. He made faces and acted the way he did during the auditions. Everyone cheered. I clapped too. It felt super to let him know he was good. I liked being a nice director.

# Chapter 13

# Better and Better

"You weren't a very good director today," Krystal whispered to me while we stood in the milk line.

My mouth dropped open.

Then her mouth turned up at the corners. "You were great."

I smiled back. "Thanks," I muttered. I could hardly say it.

I bit at my lip. "You . . . um . . . you sang

'Somewhere Over the Rainbow' really nicely on Friday, Krystal."

Krystal glowed. "Thank you, Director Ashley."

I grinned. It felt good to be with her again. Krystal was still my best pal. She stuck by me no matter what, even after I was mean to her.

"I want you to 'break a leg' on Thursday," Krystal went on. I smiled more brightly. She was using my compliment. "I want you to break both legs! My dad said he's coming to watch us!"

"Your dad? But he lives so far away!"

Krystal's eyes filled up with tears she was so happy. "I told him I was a Munchkin and you were the star. He said he would try his hardest to come."

Wow. I could hardly believe what she was saying. Would he really come all that way just to see a class play? I still didn't believe it, but I couldn't tell her that.

"That's great, Krystal," I answered her.

"The play will be wonderful, won't it?" She looked doubtful.

"The best," I reassured her. Then it was our turn to buy milk.

☆ ☆ ☆

When we arrived at school the next day, Mr. Cowles surprised us with some fake trees he borrowed from a theatre. Now we had a forest.

Then we got to take turns painting a spooky castle Mr. Cowles drew for us on some mural paper. I never got to paint anything in *Joseph*. This play was getting better and better.

Lots of the parents wanted to come. Even my mom was taking part of the morning off work. But the audience wasn't going to be as big as I'd hoped. Not all of the classes in the school were invited. Mr. Cowles felt the other grade threes and the grade twos should come. That was all.

I was a little disappointed, but the other kids weren't.

"I don't want a big audience!" whispered Sabrina.

"Yeah, it's too scary!" agreed Clayton.

I was shocked he would say that in front of everyone.

"A play is better with a smaller audience," I announced.

"It is?" Clayton asked.

"Sure, it's more . . . uh . . . real." I smiled at Clayton. He raised up his hand and held it there. I gave him a high five. He was ready.

The morning before the play everyone brought what they could for costumes.

"Our mom made furry ears and tails for all of the Monkeys." "Real tails!" exclaimed the twins. They looked funny.

"My mom sent real make-up!" called out Roberta. All the girls crowded around to look. The boys hid under the desks until Mr. Cowles told them to come out.

Mrs. Benny came in. "I have a surprise for the Munchkins!" she sang in a high voice. Out of a bag she plucked coloured beanie hats. One for each Munchkin. They were cute. Krystal's beanie was red. She liked it.

"My dad gave me his work clothes!" explained Clayton as he laid out an old plaid shirt and grey pants on the floor.

"Look! Look!" yelled Julia, and she scattered real hay over the clothes.

Clayton stuffed some of it down the clothes he had on. "Ahh!" he screamed, "it's too itchy!" Then he danced around the room, wiggling and scratching. Soon we were all scratching and giggling.

"Wait until you see what I brought!" announced Sabrina. She held out a box. We all waited.

One at a time she took them out.

"Ooh!"

"Ahh!"

Even the boys were impressed.

Ruby slippers. They looked like the real thing! Sabrina's sister had lent us some red jewelled shoes. They shone like mirrors. Of course they were too big, but she also sent tissue paper to stuff into the toes.

I let Krystal try them on.

"Oh, they're fantastic!" she gushed.

I could picture her singing in them. It gave me a funny feeling in my stomach. I was glad when she took them off.

Tomorrow morning was our play. I could hardly wait.

# Chapter 14

# Stage Fright?

Right after morning announcements, Mrs. Benny arrived to take the girls to the change rooms.

That's where we were to put on our costumes and make-up. The change rooms were right beside the stage. That way no one could see us before the curtain opened.

"That's the way it is done in *real* plays," explained Mr. Cowles. I nodded.

Mr. Cowles went with the boys to their change room.

"Make-up first, make-up first," sang Mrs. Benny. She seemed almost more excited than we were.

Mrs. Benny helped us put on lipstick and blusher. Mrs. Benny was really good with make-up. She made the Wicked Witch look very scary.

Our voices got higher and higher. Sabrina and Sarah were so excited, they zoomed and zipped around the room. They bumped into the other girls, making them giggle and shriek. I felt as though I were inside a pinball machine.

I gathered up my costume and ran my fingers over the ruby slippers. My stomach started making flip-flops.

I looked around for Krystal. She wasn't in the change room. I sneaked out the door into the small passageway that led to the stage. She wasn't there either. I crept up the side stairs.

There she was. She had her costume in her hand and was peeking through the big brown curtains.

"Krystal! You're not supposed to do that!" I whispered loudly.

She yanked back her head. Her eyes were shining like stars.

"He's here, he's here, he's here," she sang over and over. Krystal started to dance around the stage. She bumped into a fake tree.

I ran over to the opening and pulled the curtain apart. There was Krystal's father. He was standing at the doorway to the gym, talking to the school principal. Some other parents had arrived, too. They were starting to sit in the wooden chairs the caretaker had set up for our audience.

"He's already picked out his seat," Krystal breathed into my ear. She had stopped whirling around and now stood close beside me. "See the camcorder on the chair in the front row?"

I nodded.

"That's his! He always videotapes us on special occasions!"

Krystal started humming "Somewhere Over the Rainbow." She looked so excited I thought she would burst like a soap bubble.

I peeked back through the curtain. Lying beside the camcorder on the chair was a bunch of yellow flowers. Flowers? Ohhh. They must be for Krystal. My stomach lurched.

Flowers and a camcorder for a Munchkin? It wasn't right.

Suddenly, I pulled my head out of the curtain opening. I grabbed my stomach and bent over. "Oww!" I moaned.

"Ashley?" Krystal's voice sounded concerned, but not concerned enough.

I dropped my costume. The ruby slippers landed with a thud on the hard floor. I clutched my stomach with both hands. My moaning got louder. "*Owwww!*"

"Ashley, what is it?"

"I'm sick, Krystal, I'm so sick."

# Chapter 15

# The Show Must Go On

"What? You can't be sick! You're Dorothy. We need you. My dad came all this way to see you!"

I looked up at Krystal. Her face was white. She looked terrified.

"I can't be Dorothy," I wailed. "I'm too sick."

"Oh, no. I'll get Mr. Cowles," Krystal gasped, and she backed away.

"No, no, there's no time. Put on my costume, Krystal. You'll have to be Dorothy."

"Me?" She almost shrieked.

"Girls, what's going on back here?" said Mr. Cowles' voice from the stairs.

I held onto my stomach but didn't dare look up.

"Ashley's sick, Mr. Cowles! Really, really sick!"

"Sick?" Mr. Cowles strode up beside us. I could see his brown shoes on the wooden floor beside me. I nodded but I didn't make a sound.

I felt a hand press against my forehead.

"You have no fever, Ashley. And you were fine just a few minutes ago. What's this about?"

"I . . . I just . . . "

"She looked out at the audience and saw my father and got sick!" Krystal exclaimed. She sounded all in a flap, like Mrs. Benny.

"Calm down, Krystal. What's this about your father?"

"He drove four hours just to see us!"

"Did he now?" Mr. Cowles leaned over. I could tell he was peeking through the curtain. "Mmm. I never expected stage fright from you, Ashley Lawrence."

I clenched my jaw tight and said nothing.

"What should we do now?" Mr. Cowles asked. I felt he was asking me.

"Krystal should be Dorothy," I whispered.

Krystal gasped. "I . . . I don't think I can," she stammered.

I straightened up and looked her full in the face. "Of course you can, Krystal. You know the lines in the whole play better than anyone and you sing . . . well . . . better than anyone I know. You're a fantastic Dorothy."

"I am?" she asked.

I nodded solemnly. Then I quickly grabbed at my stomach again and glanced over at Mr. Cowles. He was watching me.

I looked down at my shoes. My costume lay there on the floor. The ruby slippers gleamed. I clutched at my shirt. I wanted to reach down and grab them. I wanted to keep them for ever and ever.

Suddenly, Mr. Cowles reached down. He picked up one slipper and then the other. Then he lifted up my costume and dusted it off.

"Better hurry and get this on, Krystal. The cast really needs you now. You'll have to save the play."

"Oh, oh, oh," was all she could manage to say. "Ashley, I . . . " she stammered.

"Hurry up," I commanded, forcing my voice to sound loud. I snatched her costume from her hands. Mr. Cowles laid Dorothy's dress over her arm and set the ruby slippers on top.

"I'll do my best for you," she whispered.

My insides grew tight.

She gripped the ruby slippers, turned and ran across the stage. She bounded down the stairs two at a time.

"Break a leg," I whispered to her. "Break everything." And I knew she would.

I pressed the Munchkin costume into my stomach. My throat hurt. I shifted from one foot to the other. No more ruby slippers. The sounds of the audience filling up the gym filtered through the curtain. I could hear laughter and talking. Soon the play would start.

I waited for Mr. Cowles to speak, but he didn't say anything. What should I do now? If I was supposed to be sick, I guess I'd have to go home. My shoulders sagged. I wouldn't even get to see Krystal be the star. My throat squeezed even tighter and my eyes stung. The star.

A hand rested on my shoulder. Mr. Cowles patted me gently.

"Well, if you're that sick, you can't very well be Krystal's Munchkin."

I shook my head. I still couldn't look at him. Was he mad at me for letting down the cast?

"Usually the director gets a front-row seat beside the producer. Yes, I think our director should be out front. Perhaps she should even introduce the play."

What was he saying?

"And the director's mother might want to sit with her too. Especially when I tell her what you did for Krystal."

Slowly, I lifted up my head. I looked into Mr. Cowles' face. He knew I wasn't sick. He knew and he wasn't mad at me. My throat felt like I was swallowing a rock.

"I really did want to be Dorothy," I said hoarsely. A tear slipped out and trickled down my cheek.

"I know that, Ashley," said Mr. Cowles quietly. Then he smiled a little. "But you do have *Joseph*. I'd like to see you in that, at least. When does it open?"

I sighed and wiped the tear from my cheek. "Two weeks today." I stared at our forest for a second. "Director Nielson apologized to us last night, you know."

"I'm glad to hear that," said Mr. Cowles and he nodded his head.

"Director Nielson said sometimes he forgets we're kids. He said he'd try to remember that for the rest of the rehearsals."

Mr. Cowles nodded again but he didn't say anything. The sounds from the audience were louder. The classes had started to arrive.

I crossed my arms over my chest, hugging the Munchkin costume tightly. "I don't know if I'll stay in *Joseph*. It's not much fun, you know."

"Mmm." Mr. Cowles sounded disappointed. "I understand."

Then he bent down so his face was closer to mine. "A professional show is hard work, Ashley, not like a class play. Most children couldn't do it."

I waited for him to say more but he just looked at me.

"Don't you think I can do it?" I asked.

Mr. Cowles smiled slightly. "I never said that, Ashley."

I studied Mr. Cowles. Then I nodded hard. I knew I could do it. I could learn more about being a director. A good one.

"Mr. Cowles," I said. "I *can* do it. I'm staying in."

"Good for you!" he said, and patted my shoulder again. "Now, we'd better get going." Slowly, we walked across the stage. At the top of the stairs he stopped and looked down at me.

"You should know, though, directing is not what you're best at."

"Oh?" I looked at him uneasily. "What am I best at?"

Mr. Cowles smiled broadly. "Being a friend, Ashley. You're *definitely* the best at that."

I imagined Krystal on stage singing "Somewhere over the Rainbow" and everyone clapping and clapping. I smiled my best smile. I felt like a shiny star.

All at once, the noise from the audience seemed to fill the whole backstage. Mr. Cowles held out his elbow and I looped my arm through his.

"It's showtime!" I boomed in my best director's voice and we marched down the stairs together.

As a professional storyteller, **Cathy Miyata** performs on stages across Ontario and around the world. She loves stories and has been writing them down since she was a young girl. Cathy is inspired by the funny things that happen to her — she writes them down in her "ho ho journal" and uses them in her work.

Cathy and her family live in Burlington, Ontario. This is her first novel.